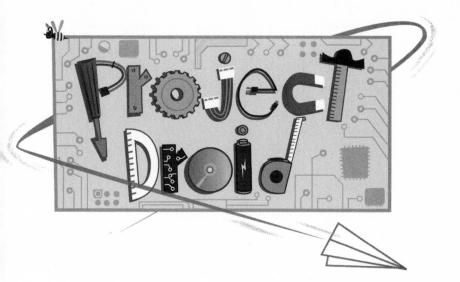

Phone-y Friends

Nancy Krulik and Amanda Burwasser

Phone-y Friends

Illustrated by Mike Moran

Sky Pony Press
New York

First Edition

This is a work of fiction. Names, characters, places, and incidents are from the authors' imaginations, and used fictitiously.

While this book aims to accurately describe the steps a child should be able to perform reasonably independently when crafting, a supervising adult should be present at all times. The authors, illustrator, and publisher take no responsibility for any injury caused while making a project from this book.

Sky Pony Press books may be purchased in bulk at special discounts for sales promotion, corporate gifts, fund-raising, or educational purposes. Special editions can also be created to specifications. For details, contact the Special Sales Department, Sky Pony Press, 307 West 36th Street, 11th Floor, New York, NY 10018 or info@skyhorsepublishing.com.

Sky Pony® is a registered trademark of Skyhorse Publishing, Inc.®, a Delaware corporation.

Visit our website at www.skyponypress.com.

www.realnancykrulik.com
www.mikemoran.net

10 9 8 7 6 5 4 3 2 1

Library of Congress Cataloging-in-Publication Data available on file.

Cover illustration by Mike Moran
Cover design by Sammy Yuen

Hardcover ISBN: 978-1-5107-2662-8
Ebook ISBN 978-1-5107-2667-3

Printed in the United States of America

Interior Design by Joshua Barnaby

For Barbara and John, ever supportive friends

—NK

For Penny, Benay, Eileen, Audra, and Leah

—AB

For John C., Arlo Guthrie fan/MOTIVATOR!

—MM

CONTENTS

1.

Lead, Schmead

"Who's next?" Mr. Fluff shouted from behind his piano bench.

"I am!" Nadine Vardez answered loudly.

Nadine climbed the stairs at the side of the stage and stood in the spotlight. She looked over at our music teacher and took a deep breath. "Ready when you are," she told him.

Mr. Fluff began playing the piano. Nadine sang along with the music.

As she sang, my stomach got all twisted up in knots.

Like most of the other kids who had gathered in the school auditorium, Nadine was trying out for our school play, *Hansel and Gretel.*

The rest of us were waiting for our turn to go up there on stage and give it our best.

And Nadine was only two people ahead of me in line.

Which meant that any minute now, it would be *my* turn to go up there, stand in the middle of the stage, and try out.

Gulp.

I had never been center stage before.

I had never acted before.

And I had *definitely* never danced in front of anyone before.

But now I was going to have to sing and act and dance in front of Mr. Fluff, Nadine, and a whole of bunch of other kids.

Thump. Thump. Thump. My heart was pounding hard.

I felt a little sick.

My palms were all sweaty.

And if I wasn't nervous enough, the snobbiest kids in school, the Silverspoon twins, were trying out for the play, too. *They* weren't one bit nervous. And they were making sure everyone knew it.

"We're definitely going to get the parts of Hansel and Gretel," Sherry bragged. "After all, we're twins."

"Our father hired us a singing coach," Jerry added. "And a tap dancing teacher. We are going to get the lead parts."

"I wouldn't be so sure," I told them. "Nadine is really good. And my audition is going to knock your socks off!"

"I CAN DO IT!"

Just then, my cousin Java sprang out from the crowd of kids. He kicked off his shoes and yanked off his socks. Then he smiled at me. "I knocked *my* socks off," he said. "And my shoes, too."

A bunch of kids laughed and pointed at him.

Oh boy, I thought. *Here we go again.*

I really wished my cousin would just act like a normal kid.

But how could he? He *wasn't* normal.

Or a kid.

He was an android.

My mom is a scientist. She likes to build things. So she built me a robot cousin. His name is **J**acob **A**lexander **V**ictor **A**pplebaum. But I just call him Java.

My mom and I are the only ones who know that Java isn't a real kid. And we can't let anyone else know. That's because he's part of her secret scientific project: **Project Droid**.

The whole point of Project Droid is to figure out if an android can fit in with real people. So Java is programmed to do all sorts of real kid things—like go to school and play soccer and try out for the school play.

Only, he doesn't always do those things the same way a real kid would.

And he doesn't always understand what real kids are talking about.

Which is why he was now standing in the middle of the auditorium without his socks and shoes.

"Java!" Mr. Fluff shouted from the stage. "It's your turn. Let's see how well you can dance."

My android cousin ran, barefoot, up onto the stage.

"Java, where are your shoes?" Mr. Fluff asked him.

Java didn't answer. He just stared at our music teacher with the goofy grin he always has on his face.

"That's how all the kids dance where Java comes from," I said quickly. I didn't add that Java *really* came from my mother's lab in our house.

Mr. Fluff sat down at the piano. He began to play a silly-sounding song.

Java started to dance a jolly jig.

He kicked his left foot forward. He swung his right foot back.

He turned around in a circle. Then he twirled around again.

And again.

And again.

He was twirling faster.

And faster.

And fas—

THUD.

Java twirled himself right off the stage.

Sherry looked at him and laughed. "Your cousin is a rotten dancer."

"It's like he's got two left feet," Jerry said. He laughed so hard, he snorted.

Java looked up at the twins and shook his head. "No, I don't," he said. "This one is a right foot. Logan's mom made sure I have one of each."

The twins stared at him. Then they stared at me.

I rolled my eyes. Java sure didn't make keeping his secret easy.

2.

Don't Be a Blockhead

"Mom!" I shouted excitedly as I ran into the house after school the next day. "I got one! I got a part in the play!"

Mom came running out of her lab. She lifted her goggles and smiled. "Which part?" she asked.

"I'm Chipmunk Number Three!" I said proudly. "Mr. Fluff told me I was perfect for the part because I can blow up my cheeks really big."

I took a deep breath and then blew into my cheeks until they looked like two giant balloons.

Mom smiled. "You're going to be the best chipmunk on that stage," she told me proudly. Then she turned to Java.

"What part did you get?" she asked him.

"I did not get a part," Java replied.

I looked over at Java. I expected him to look sad or upset. But he didn't. He had the same goofy smile on his face that he always had.

I guess robots don't *get* sad.

"Do you want to play now, Logan?" Java asked as he followed me up the stairs and into my room. "We can throw a baseball. Or kick around a soccer ball."

"I can't today, Java," I told him. "I have *a* line to memorize."

Java started to walk slowly out of my room.

I felt terrible. Java didn't have a line to memorize or a song to practice. He didn't have anything to do.

"Maybe we can play ball together later," I told him. "Why don't you do something else for a little while?"

"Like what?" Java asked me.

"I don't know," I said. "Anything. Maybe take a walk around the block?"

"I CAN DO IT!" Java shouted out loudly.

Before I knew what was happening, Java raced over to my toy chest.

He yanked out my busted tennis racket, two action figures, and an old stuffed bunny that was missing an eye and part of its tail. Finally, he pulled out a wooden, purple block.

"Found it!" he exclaimed as he placed the block on the floor, and walked around it in a circle.

"Okay," Java said happily. "I walked around the block. Can we play now?"

There was no arguing with my robot cousin.

"Okay, Java," I said, laughing. "Let's go play. I guess I can memorize my line later."

3.

Dive Right In

"Where are we, Hansel?"

Nadine's voice carried through the whole auditorium at rehearsal after school the next day. She had already memorized *all* of her lines.

That was a big deal because Nadine was playing Gretel, so she had a lot of lines.

I hadn't even memorized my *one* line. Java had kept me too busy playing ball to learn it.

I watched as the Silverspoon twins slithered onto the stage and got ready for the next scene. They were covered in glue, branches, apples, and leaves.

"Why are you two in costume?"
Mr. Fluff asked the twins. "This isn't a
dress rehearsal."

"We're getting into character," Jerry said.

"That's what *real* actors do," Sherry
added.

"If we are going to *play* trees," Jerry
explained. "We have to *become* trees."

"Yuck! There's a bug in these leaves!"
Sherry complained. "It just crawled up
my nose. *Aachoo!*"

I laughed as the creepy crawly went
flying out of one of her nostrils.

"Hey, Logan,"
said Leah, a
fifth grader who
was playing a gopher.

"Why is your cousin at rehearsal? I saw the cast list. His name's not there. He's not in the play."

I looked to the back of the auditorium. Sure enough, there was Java, sitting in one of the seats, staring into space.

"He's waiting to ride the late bus home with me," I explained.

"Couldn't he have gone home by himself?" Leah asked.

How was I supposed to answer that? Java didn't do *anything* on his own.

"He's still new to the school," I finally said. "We go pretty much everywhere together."

Leah started to say something, but Mr. Fluff interrupted her.

"Okay animals, gather around," he called out. "It's time to rehearse the candy house song and dance."

We animals all scurried onto the stage with our scripts in our hands.

Mr. Fluff played the piano, and we sang.

Gingerbread roof and marshmallow walls.
Caramel rugs, chewy bathroom stalls.
You can eat the sink and lick the ceiling.
A sugary rush is the very best feeling.

As we finished our song and dance, Mr. Fluff clapped excitedly. "Children," he said, "that went swimmingly!"

Just then, from the back of the auditorium, I heard Java shout, **"I CAN DO IT!"**

My cousin dropped to his stomach in the middle of the aisle, and began moving his arms and legs like he was doing the front crawl.

I turned to look at Java, and my jaw dropped open with surprise.

I shut it quick, before a bug from Sherry's costume could fly into my mouth.

"What's he doing?" Leah asked me.

I didn't answer. I had no idea.

"I'm going *swimmingly*," Java told us proudly. Then he flipped over onto his back. "I can do the backstroke." He turned onto his side. "And the sidestroke."

"Your cousin is ruining the whole rehearsal," Jerry hissed at me.

"Yeah," Sherry agreed. "You have to get him out of here."

For once, I agreed with Sherry and Jerry.

I really wished my cousin would just make like a tree and leave.

4.

Not Having a Ball

The evil witch has a wart on her nose.
And a slimy green fungus that grows on
her toes . . .

The next day, my new theater friends
and I spent recess together. Instead of
playing, like we usually would, we sat

around a picnic table practicing the songs from our show.

The witch smells like old socks, and she's got chicken pox.

Her gray hair looks fried. She's got a lumpy backside.

As we sang, I looked across the playground. Java was heading my way. For some reason—or *no* reason—he was flapping his arms up and down.

I was afraid he might suddenly take off like a bird, so I hurried over to stop him. "What are you doing that for?" I asked my cousin.

"Hi, Logan." Java smiled. "Do you want to play birdman with me?"

Why would I want to do that?

"I can't play with you right now," I said. "I'm hanging out with my friends from the play. You need to find your own friends."

"What friends?" Java asked. "Like Stanley?"

I shook my head. "Stanley is *my* friend. And right now, he's hanging out with kids from the photography club."

"Well, who then?" Java asked.

"I don't know," I told him. "Find someone you have stuff in common with."

As I walked back to the table where the show kids were hanging out, I saw Java looking around the playground. Everyone else seemed to be busy playing with their own groups of friends.

My cousin was left all alone.

He walked over to the empty volleyball court and picked up the ball.

Slap! Java served the ball over the net.

Whoosh! He slid under the net, just in time to slap the ball back over to the other side.

Whoosh!

Slap!

Whoosh!

Java was diving back and forth under the net, hitting the ball at robotic top speed.

Kids came from all over the playground to watch my cousin play volleyball by himself. They thought he looked cool.

But I thought he looked sad. And lonely.

Which was weird. Because Java *never* looked sad.

And I didn't think it was possible for a droid to ever feel lonely.

But maybe I was wrong.

5.

Sing Your Hard Drive Out

"Logan, I want you to meet my new friend," Java said that evening. He and I were hanging out in the living room while mom was in the kitchen making dinner.

I looked around the room. "There's no one here," I said.

"Sure there is." Java picked up my mom's smartphone and pushed a button.

"Hello, Spike," he said.

"Hello, Java," the phone said back.

"It is good to hear your voice," Java replied. He looked at me. "Spike is my new friend."

I laughed. "Java, that's a cell phone. It can't be your friend."

But Java wasn't listening to me. He was too busy talking to Spike.

"I have a new joke for you," Java told the phone. "Do you know why the robot was angry?"

"No," the phone said. "Why?"

"Because someone kept pushing his buttons," Java answered. "Isn't that a funny joke?"

"It is very funny," Spike answered.

I couldn't believe my ears. Java was having a conversation with my mother's phone.

"Do *you* know any jokes, Spike?" Java asked.

"Sure," Spike replied. "What is a robot's favorite type of music?"

"I know that one," Java answered. "Heavy metal."

"Yes," Spike said. "And here is some music just for you."

Suddenly, some really loud music started to blast out of my mom's smartphone. Java began to dance around the room as he listened to the heavy drumbeat.

He swiveled his hips to the left.

He twisted his hips to the right.

Then he banged his head against the wall to the sound of the beat.

When the music stopped, Java smiled at the phone. "That was fun," he said. "Now here is a music joke for you. What is a smartphone's favorite kind of music?"

"A sym-phone-y!" Spike replied.

"Yes!" Java started to laugh. Well, a robot kind of laugh, anyway.

I thought I heard my mother's phone laughing, too.

Which was really strange.

I didn't know phones could laugh.

But then I didn't know robots could tell jokes, either!

Oh brother. This was getting to be too much. I flopped down on the couch.

"Are you okay, Logan?" Java asked.

"I'm just tired from rehearsal. Being in a play is hard work. I'm singing and dancing my heart out up there on stage."

Java dropped the phone. "**I CAN DO IT!**" he shouted.

He looked down at his chest and started to peel off his shirt. Then he stopped.

"I *can't* do it," he admitted in a small, sad voice. "I don't have a heart. But I

can sing and dance my hard drive out
if you want." He began to unscrew his
belly button so he could take out his hard
drive.

Uh oh.

"That's okay, Java," I said, grabbing his
hand to stop him. "It's probably better if
you sing with your hard drive *in*."

"Good idea, Logan," Java said. He picked up the phone and pushed the button. "Spike, do you know any robot songs?" he asked.

Spike began to sing:

I am a robot, metal and strong.

I never sleep. I think all day long.

Robots are powerful. Robots are smart.

We are beautiful metal works of art.

"That's what friends are for," Java said with a smile. Then he joined in. "*I am a robot, metal and strong. I never sleep. I think all day long . . .*"

I looked at my cousin and his new friend and shook my head. Java had done some strange things since Mom first built him. But making friends with a phone might just have been the strangest thing yet.

6.

A Group of Gadgets

"Do you kids want a snack?" Mom asked as my theater friends and I walked into the house after rehearsal a few days later. "I can make tuna and blueberry sandwiches if you'd like. Great brain food. It will help you memorize your lines."

My new friends looked grossed out.

"How about some cookies?" I suggested to Mom.

"Okay," she said. "There are oatmeal raisin cookies in the cupboard. Go ahead into the kitchen. Java is already in there—with *his* new friends."

His new what?

I had no idea Java had made any friends other than Spike. I'd been too busy with the show to notice that he'd been hanging out with anybody new lately.

I wondered what sort of kids would want to hang out with Java.

"Come on," I said to my castmates as I walked into the kitchen. "We have juice boxes and—"

I stopped mid-sentence and gaped in surprise. There was Java, sitting on the floor, surrounded by kitchen appliances.

"Look, Logan!" he called to me. "I found friends I have stuff in common with. We all have motors and gears!"

My theater friends started laughing.

"What's up with your cousin?" Dylan, the kid who was playing Hansel, asked me.

"Java, you're so funny," Nadine giggled. "What are you doing down there?"

"I am playing with my friends." Java smiled. He looked really happy.

Nadine laughed harder. "You're hilarious," she told him. "Always kidding around."

I had a feeling Java wasn't kidding at all. Just a few nights ago he'd been singing along with my mother's phone.

But I didn't say that.

I figured it was better to let my friends think this was all one big Java joke.

Just then, I noticed the dishwasher was overflowing. "You put too much soap in there," I told my cousin.

But Java didn't care. He just kept grinning his goofy grin.

"I love blowing bubbles, too, Dishy-Washy," Java told the dishwasher. "Watch!"

Java took a deep breath and blew into the soap bubbles.

He blew.

And blew.

And blew.

The bubble kept growing.

And growing.

And growing.

It grew until it was practically as big as the whole kitchen! And then—

Soap suds splattered all over my new theater friends and me.

Java didn't seem to notice that we were covered in soap. He reached over and clicked a button on the electric mixer.

The mixing bowl started spinning around and around.

So Java started spinning around and around, too.

"This is fun, Mixy!" Java sang out as he spun faster and faster.

"He's gonna get really dizzy doing that," Leah said.

I was pretty sure Leah meant that Java would get dizzy, not Mixy. Not that it mattered. Mixers don't get dizzy. And neither do droids.

Java spun his way over to the refrigerator. His elbow bashed into the water dispenser on the door. Water shot out onto the floor. It looked like the refrigerator was peeing.

"Good idea, Chilly!" Java exclaimed.

Uh oh.

I didn't think robots could pee. But why take a chance?

"Mom!" I shouted. "You gotta stop him. **NOW!**"

7.

I See, You Saw

"Hello, Logan," Java greeted me as I walked backstage before rehearsal the following day.

"Hi, Java," I said. "Are you having fun building the scenery?"

"I am helping to build the witch's house," Java told me.

"That's good," I said. "Just try not to cause any trouble, okay?"

"Trouble is a bad thing, Logan. Why would I want to cause that?"

I didn't answer him. Java never *meant* to cause trouble. But that didn't mean he didn't cause any.

In fact, he caused trouble all the time.

As Java went back to work, the Silverspoons hurried over to me. It wasn't easy for them to hurry, since they were wearing so many branches, leaves, and apples on their heads.

"What's your crazy cousin doing here?" Jerry asked me.

"Shouldn't he be home playing with the hair dryer or something?"

Sherry sniped nastily.

I frowned. One of my new friends must have told the twins about Java's playdate in the kitchen. By now, everyone in the whole cast probably knew about it.

"My mom thought it would be good for Java to be part of the play," I told them.

"He's building sets and painting scenery."

I looked nervously over at my cousin. *Please, please, please don't do anything weird,* I thought to myself.

Java was busy screwing two parts of the house frame together. *Phew.* That wasn't weird at all. Except . . .

Uh oh.

Java wasn't using a *screwdriver.* He was using his *fingernail* to turn the screw. His whole hand was spinning around and around.

Luckily, the twins didn't seem to have noticed. I guess all the leaves and apples in front of their faces made it hard for them to see.

But it wasn't hard for them to *hear*. Java was whistling really loud.

"Hey, Java?" Jerry called over to him.

Java smiled and stopped working. "Hello, Jerry," he said. "Hello, Sherry."

"Why were you whistling?" Sherry asked him.

"Because I am working," Java told her. "You are supposed to whistle while you work. I saw it in a movie that my friend, Telly TV, showed me."

"Your *friend*, the TV?" Jerry laughed.

"Telly?" Sherry giggled. "Your TV has a name?"

"Doesn't everybody?" Java asked her.

He sounded really curious. Like he was comparing what Sherry had just said to the information in his hard drive.

Which, of course, was exactly what he was doing.

I really wished the twins would stop talking to Java. And that he would stop answering them.

"Java, shouldn't you go back to work?" I suggested.

"Oh, yes. I need to cut another piece of wood."

Buzz. Buzz. Buzz. Java began sawing. And he stopped whistling. Which was a good thing.

Or maybe not.

Java had stopped whistling because he was sawing *with his mouth*. His teeth were like little sharp blades cutting into the wood. You can't whistle when your mouth is full of sawdust.

Gulp.

What if someone saw him sawing like that? Quickly, I leaped in front of my cousin, blocking him from view.

But I was too late.

"Did you see what I saw?" I heard Jerry ask Sherry.

"Did you see how he sawed?" Sherry asked Jerry.

"I saw. I saw," they both said.

Double gulp. The twins were sure to figure out Java's secret now! I had to say something. *Anything.*

"Our doctor told Java he needed more fiber in his diet," I told them quickly. "There's a lot of fiber in wood. Haven't you ever heard of fiberboard?"

Jerry shook his head. "I bet your dentist is going to be really mad at him."

"Our dentist gets mad when I eat a chewy caramel," Sherry told me.

Wow. Maybe the Silverspoon twins weren't as smart as I thought they were.

"Okay, everyone," Mr. Fluff called out as he walked into the auditorium. "Let's get started with rehearsal. Can the animals and the trees take their places, please?"

The other animals and I walked over to the middle of the stage. The Silverspoon twins stood in the back and raised their branches.

"Can you guys working on the sets and scenery keep it down, please?" Mr. Fluff called backstage.

The kids who were painting scenery and building sets got very quiet. Well, all the kids except—

"**I CAN DO IT**!" Java shouted suddenly. He dropped to the ground with a *thud*.

"See?" he told Mr. Fluff proudly. "I can keep it down. *All* the way down."

Some of the kids started laughing. But I didn't. I didn't think there was anything funny about Java.

The kids in the play were my new friends. I wanted them to like me. And they had started to.

But now *Java* was going to be at all the rehearsals. Which probably meant I was going to be known as Chipmunk Number Three, the kid with the weird cousin who ate wood.

Java was ruining everything.

8.

The Dance of the Animals

"I don't know what you're so nervous about," I told Leah on the night of our dress rehearsal. "Doing this show tomorrow night will be a piece of cake."

"You're not nervous at all?" she asked me, biting her nails.

"Nope," I said proudly. "I know my line. And, I've been practicing all the songs and dances."

Leah and I were standing backstage, watching Nadine and Dylan rehearse a scene with the fifth grader who was playing the Wicked Witch.

While we were waiting for our turn to go on, Leah pulled nervously at her gopher costume. But I was cool and calm.

"You mean Hansel and I can eat the whole house?" I heard Nadine say.

"Of course," the Wicked Witch answered. "Come inside with me."

That was my cue. I hurried onto the stage with the other woodland critters.

"Look, there's a boy and a girl!" I shouted my line loud and strong.

"They're going into the witch's house," one of the rabbits said.

"They'll be sorry," added the turtle.

Mr. Fluff began playing the piano. All of the animals started to sing and dance.

Deep in the woods is where she lives.

She's always angry and never forgives.

We forest animals stay safe, tucked away.

When the wicked witch comes out to play.

You silly girl, you silly boy.

Her candy house is just a ploy.

As sure as a flower has a petal

The witch will eat Hansel and Gretel.

When the song ended, I blew up my chipmunk cheeks really, really big. Then I scurried offstage with the other animals.

"See?" I said to Leah. "I told you it would be easy. No reason to be nervous at all."

At the end of the rehearsal, Mr. Fluff stood up behind his piano. "Now, children, when the show is over we will take our bows. Let's practice the curtain call."

Just then, I heard a loud shout coming from backstage.

"**I CAN DO IT**!" Java hollered. He got down on his knees and started calling, "Here curtain! Here curtain, curtain!"

"What's your cousin doing now?" Sherry asked me.

I had no idea.

"Here curtain, curtain!" Java called again, louder this time.

"I think he's calling the curtain." Jerry said.

The twins started giggling.

I felt my face getting very hot. I was glad my cheeks were covered with my chipmunk makeup. That way, no one could tell how badly Java had embarrassed me.

Again.

9.

A Logan-sicle

"Look, there's a boy and a girl," I said in an English accent.

"Look, there's a boy and a girl," I said in a French accent.

"Look, there's a boy and a girl," I said in an Armenian accent.

I was standing backstage on the night of the show practicing my one line. Java was backstage, too, waiting to open the curtains for the "Dance of the Animals" scene.

"Java, can you grab a bottle of water for me?" I asked him. "Actors cannot be parched on stage. And I am very parched."

Parched had been our vocabulary Word-for-Today a few weeks ago. I knew it meant thirsty. I also knew I could have just said *thirsty*. But parched sounded so much more actor-y.

Java reached into the ice bucket and pulled out a bottle of water. "Here you go, Logan," he said.

I took a sip and practiced my line again. "Look, there's a boy and a girl," I said in an old man's voice.

"Look," I said in a baby's voice. "There's a—"

But before I could finish practicing my line again, I heard the witch say to Hansel and Gretel, "Come inside with me."

That was my cue. I ran onstage with the other animals. I opened my mouth to say my line . . .

And nothing came out.

Not a word.

Not even a sound.

I started to sweat so badly, I could smell my own pits.

I couldn't move. I couldn't even breathe.

All I could do was stare out into that big, crowded audience.

"Oh, no," I heard somebody backstage shout. "He's got stage fright."

"It's like Logan's frozen!" somebody else added.

The next thing I heard was . . .

"I CAN DO IT!"

Out of the corner of my eye, I saw Java reach into the cooler and pull out a huge block of solid ice.

He put it in his mouth and started chewing on it. He turned the ice around and around in his mouth. Then he spit out a perfectly carved, Logan-shaped popsicle.

A *Logan*-sicle.

"It's a frozen Logan," I heard him tell the kids standing backstage.

"Say your line," Leah whispered to me. She nudged me hard in the side.

But I *couldn't* say my line. I couldn't remember it. I couldn't remember anything. My mind was blank.

And then, from the side of the stage I heard Java whisper, "Look, there's a boy and a girl."

That was my line! Now I remembered what I was supposed to say.

So I said it. *In a perfect chipmunk voice.* "Look, there's a boy and a girl."

Phew. I took a deep breath and smiled. I knew I could do it. Piece of cake.

Okay, maybe it hadn't exactly been a piece of cake. In fact, if it hadn't been for Java, it would have been a disaster.

For once, I was really happy to have had my cousin nearby.

10.

A Round of Applause

"Time for the curtain call," Mr. Fluff announced from behind his piano.

The show was over. There was nothing left for us to do but to take our bows. All the actors in the show ran out onstage.

I started to follow them. Then I stopped and grabbed Java's hand. I dragged him out there on the stage with me.

The other kids who had been working on stage followed behind him.

My cousin deserved some applause, too. When he'd whispered my line to me, he saved the show. Or at least my part of it.

"What are you bringing *them* out for?" Sherry whispered angrily.

"The curtain call is only for the actors," Jerry added.

"The kids who work backstage deserve applause, too," I argued. "Java was really important tonight. I think everybody should give him a hand."

"**I CAN DO IT!**" Java shouted. He started to unscrew his hand from his wrist. "Do you want me to give you a hand, Logan?"

I definitely did *not* want him to give me his hand—not in front of the whole audience. So I grabbed his hand and held it tightly in place.

And then, together, my cousin and I took our bows.

"We did it, Java!" I cheered.

"Yes, we did, Logan," Java added.

My cousin and I had worked really hard. We had helped make the show a real success.

We bowed again.

"Come on, folks," Mr. Fluff shouted to the audience. "Let's give them another big round of applause."

"I CAN DO IT!" Java shouted out again.

Uh oh. What now?

Java yanked his hand away from mine. He started clapping and moving his arms in a big round circle.

I laughed. That was actually pretty funny.

Some of the other kids started laughing, too. They began moving their clapping hands around in circles.

Soon, everyone in the theater was giving us another round of applause—*Java-style.*

I looked over at my cousin and grinned. I was really happy about how tonight had turned out for Java and me. We were superstars! *Both of us.*

I guess my robot cousin and I really do have have something in common, after all.

There's a Chipmunk in Your Closet!

Okay, maybe it's not a *real* chipmunk.

But if you have an old brown glove, some thread and a wooden bead lying around in your coat closet, you have the makings of a very chipper chipmunk toy!

Here's what you will need:

- ⚙ 1 brown wool glove
- ⚙ Polyester toy stuffing
- ⚙ 2 pipe cleaners (You'll cut 1 of these in half.)
- ⚙ 2 spools of embroidery thread (one black, one brown)
- ⚙ 1 black or brown wooden bead
- ⚙ 1 black fabric pen
- ⚙ Sewing pins
- ⚙ 1 sewing needle
- ⚙ 1 pair of scissors
- ⚙ 1 handy-dandy adult to help you out
- ⚙ Optional: Orange, white, and dark brown thread for decoration.

1 Brown Wool Grove

Polyester Toy Stuffing

2 Pipe cleaners
(You'll cut one in half)

2 Spools of
embroidery thread

ooden Bead

Fabric Pen

Handy-Dandy
Adult

wing Needle

Sewing Pins

Scissors

Here's what you do:

1 Turn the glove inside-out.

2 Use the fabric pen to label the parts of the chipmunk on the inside of the glove. The picture will show you how to draw the parts onto the glove. Make sure you copy both the dotted lines and the solid ones.

3 Ask an adult to help you cut out each part of the chipmunk. Cut only on the solid lines.

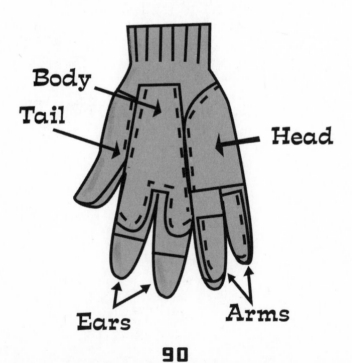

4 Pin both sides of each chipmunk part together.

5 Use brown thread to sew the tail, body, head, and arms along the dotted lines. (You might want to have an adult help you with all the sewing.)

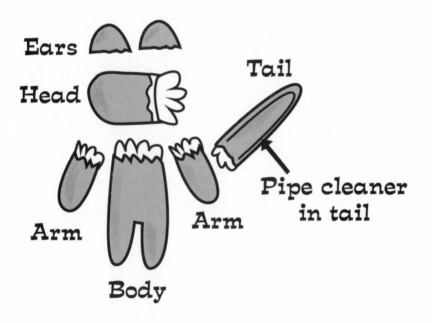

Ears

Head

Tail

Arm

Arm

Pipe cleaner in tail

Body

6 Once they are sewn together, flip each of the body parts right-side-out.

7 Bend the pipe cleaners into U-shapes. Insert one of the smaller pipe cleaner U-shapes into each of the legs.

8 Insert the long pipe-cleaner U-shape into the tail.

9 Stuff the legs, tail, body, head, and arms of your chipmunk. Do not stuff the ears.

Sew the body, arms, and tail shut. Make sure to leave a ¼-inch border on each piece.

Fold the ¼-inch border in on each piece and stitch it up.

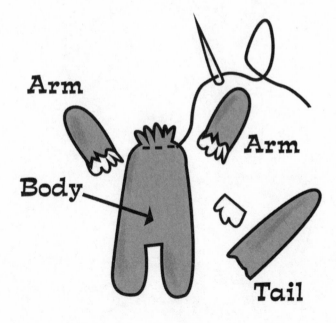

12 Fold the back of the chipmunk's head in this order: left, right, bottom, top. Then sew the head shut.

Back of head

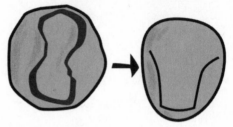

 13 Insert the openings of the ears into the back of the chipmunk's head and sew them on.

Front   **Back**

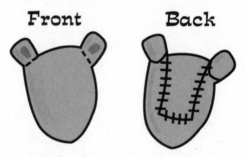

If you'd like to decorate the tail, sew small, evenly spaced stitches along the tail in orange, white, and dark brown thread to create stripes.

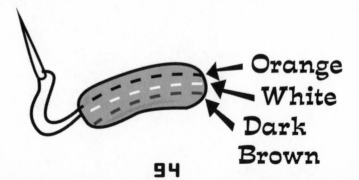

Orange
White
Dark
Brown

Sew the arms, tail, and head onto the chipmunk's body.

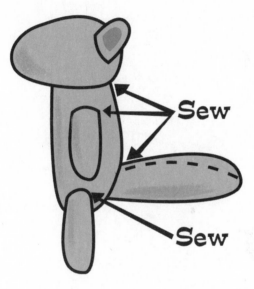

Sew

Sew

 Make one black thread stitch for each of the chipmunk's eyes.

16

Sew the wooden bead onto the chipmunk's face to make his nose.

Template

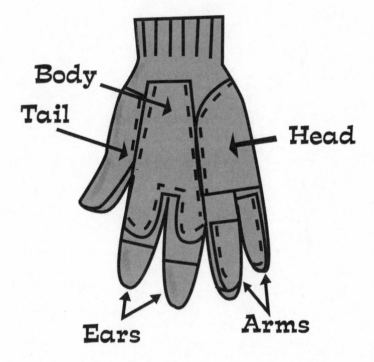

About the Authors

Nancy Krulik is the author of more than two hundred books for children and young adults including three *New York Times* bestsellers and the popular Katie Kazoo, Switcheroo; George Brown, Class Clown; and Magic Bone series. She lives in New York City with her husband and a crazy beagle mix. Visit her online at www.realnancykrulik.com.

Amanda Burwasser holds a BFA with honors in creative writing from Pratt Institute in New York City. Her senior thesis earned the coveted Pratt Circle Award. A preschool teacher, she resides in Forestville, California.

About the Illustrator

Mike Moran is a dad, husband, and illustrator. His illustrations can be seen in children's books, animation, magazines, games, World Series programs, and more. He lives in Florham Park, New Jersey. Visit him online at www.mikemoran.net.

GET OVERJOYED FOR MORE DROID!

Project Droid #1: Science No Fair!

When you have an android cousin, losing your head takes on a whole new meaning.

Project Droid #2: Soccer Shocker!

The Purple Wombats' secret weapon has a really big secret.

Project Droid #3:

My Robot Ate My Homework

How in the world can Logan get out of

this mess?